≠
N711w

Wolf Child

Dennis Nolan

Macmillan Publishing Company · New York

Collier Macmillan Publishers · London

A special thanks to Owen, Jessie, and Lauren
for helping the past come alive.
Thank you to Dr. Francine Bradley, Cynthia Book,
Jean and Rudy Zallinger, Ann Turner, and my writing group
for helping me to maintain accuracy
and refine the manuscript.

For information about wolf recovery programs,
contact the Defenders of Wildlife,
1244 Nineteenth Street NW,
Washington, DC 20036,
and the Canadian Wolf Defenders,
Box 3480, Station D,
Edmonton, Alberta T5L 4J3.

Macmillan Publishing Company, 866 Third Avenue, New York, NY 10022
Collier Macmillan Canada, Inc.
First Edition   Printed in the United States of America

10   9   8   7   6   5   4   3   2   1

The text of this book is set in 12 point Meridien.
The illustrations are rendered in watercolor.

Library of Congress Cataloging-in-Publication Data
Nolan, Dennis.
Wolf Child/written and illustrated by Dennis Nolan.
—1st ed.   p.   cm.
Summary: Too weakened by illness to be a hunter, nine-year-old Teo
is apprenticed to the toolmaker Mova but leads a lonely existence
until he finds and befriends an orphaned wolf cub. But food is
scarce and the leader of the clan is against keeping the animal.
ISBN 0-02-768141-6
[1. Man, Prehistoric—Fiction. 2. Wolves—Fiction.] I. Title.
PZ7.N678Wo   1989   [Fic]—dc19   88-35955   CIP   AC

For Richard Stiller

and days long ago

Long ago when the world was young, the wind raced down the mountains and through the valleys. Snow covered the earth, and it was winter everywhere. Inside the cave the first fire burned brightly, but the wind howled outside, seeking to get in.

Teo pulled his robe tightly about him as the icy wind bit at his fingers. Like a lone eagle, he sat, high atop his rocky perch, tired and bored after a morning of searching for stones. He listened to the wind's lonely cry as it blew past him and whistled through the valley below.

I wish the wind were my friend, he thought. Then we could fly to the Ice Mountain and run with the horses. He imagined himself soaring over the Ice Mountain, the great glacier that filled the valleys to the north and sent winds howling over the frozen earth. We could race through the tall grass of the slope and rest in the trees, like the white owl. But now I must stay here, like this stone.

Teo held up a perfect piece of obsidian. He had been lucky. Obsidian was the favorite of toolmakers, but it was hard to find. Weighing it in his hand, he looked for the long, sharp spearhead he could chip from it. He remembered Mova's words: *The black stones are the best. They have all the tools inside.*

A month ago, when the winter snows had melted, old Mova, the toolmaker, had taken Teo as an apprentice. Teo's father had died on a hunt high in the mountains when Teo was just a year old. Now Teo was nine, too old to gather roots and herbs with the women and children, but five winters of sickness · had left him too weak ever to be a hunter.

At first Teo was happy being left alone while the others searched for food. He learned to make hand axes and scrapers and knife blades. He learned what the perfect stone looked like and where to find it. But Mova was poor company, always turning his silent attention to his work. "You must listen for the song of the stones," Mova would say. "The stones are your friends."

"I have no friends," said Teo angrily, and threw the piece of obsidian down the cliff. He watched it bounce and disappear among the rocks below. "I hate being a toolmaker."

A cold blast of wind licked at his ears, and again he wished it could take him flying over the gleaming white snows. Then he heard a high-pitched squeal, and a chill shot down his spine. "Mova! Mova!" he called as he reached for his digging stick. They had wandered high into the hills today, far from the protection of the cave, and the mountains were full of dangerous predators—cave lions, snow leopards, and hyenas. Again he called for Mova, but only the wind answered. Teo shivered and squinted his eyes to search the rocks, the wind died, and all was still.

Then Teo heard the sound again. It was the whimpering cry of a young animal. He scrambled across the rocks, following the sound to a small hole in the hillside, and jumped back as a tiny gray animal stumbled out. "A wolf child," said Teo, and he pulled the cub from the shadows. He laughed as it wiggled in his hands and licked at his face, unafraid. Teo petted its soft fur and held it close. In the hollow of the rocks they were protected from the wind. The cub was lying quietly in his lap when Teo heard Mova's voice echoing over the hill.

"I am here! I am all right!" Teo shouted as Mova climbed down to the sheltered den. "Look, Mova," he said, holding up the cub, "a wolf child. I heard it calling me."

"It is just hungry," said Mova gruffly. "Like all children." Mova took the cub gently in his leathery hands. It blinked in the bright sunlight and whined softly. "A she-wolf," he said. "Very young." He handed her back and looked sternly at Teo. "I told you to be careful. The mountains are full of dangers. You should not enter a wolf's den alone." He poked inside the den with his spear, then walked to the cliff edge to scan the hillsides. The only movement was an eagle circling slowly above the valley on the wind currents. "A wolf is always near its child," said Mova. "This one must be an orphan."

"Can I keep her, Mova?" asked Teo, holding the cub tightly. Mova frowned.

"She is all alone. She is just a baby, and you said she was hungry. I will take care of her. Can I keep her?" Teo begged.

"Only Ohnka can decide," said Mova finally. "It is time to go." He turned and walked down the hillside toward the cave. Teo picked up his heavy leather bag of stones and followed, but his step was light with the wolf cub cuddled in his arms.

Mova was silent the rest of the afternoon, carefully arranging his stones in piles, separating them by size and shape. Teo sat quietly near the entrance of the large cave, keeping the wolf cub warm in a bearskin, waiting for the others to return.

The women came first, a dozen of them, with five children. Two babies were carried close inside their mothers' robes. Teo saw them at the far end of the valley, their long shadows stretching out in the late afternoon sun. Mother will know how to feed the wolf child, thought Teo as he watched the women climb the steep hill, carrying their sacks of early spring herbs and flowers. He heard their laughter and singing and remembered happy days spent gathering summer berries in the flowering meadows.

"Mother, Mother," Teo called excitedly. "I have a wolf child." Proudly he showed the squirming bundle of gray fur to the children as they crowded around. Reena, Teo's mother, looked first at Mova, who did not stir from his work, and then at Teo.

"We cannot bring animals to the cave," she said. "You must take this one away before Ohnka returns."

"But she is hungry," said Teo.

The wolf cub wiggled from his lap and scampered about the rock floor, tripping over her own feet. The children giggled as she sniffed at their toes, tickling them with her wet nose.

Reena bent down and picked up the cub. "She *is* hungry." Reena laughed as the cub whined and licked at her face. "I will feed her—for now," she said. "And wait for Ohnka."

Teo was glad his mother had arrived before Ohnka. With his rough low voice and his piercing gaze, the tall leader of the small band of thirty had always frightened Teo. A strong, brave hunter, Ohnka would lead the men to the tundra each day in search of game. Always on the lookout for the fierce giant cats of the glaciers, Ohnka would bark his commands to the men as they chased after mountain goats, the ibex, or the chamois. More often they would settle for a catch of lemmings or rabbits plucked from their burrows in the frozen slopes.

Teo followed Reena into the cave, to the fire still smoldering from the morning meal. Mixing herbs, shredded meat, and water, she soon had a hot broth boiling over the coals. Tiny needlelike teeth nipped at Teo as he offered the cub small pieces of meat and let her lick the broth from his fingers. Finally her hunger was satisfied. She settled into Teo's lap as Reena petted her softly.

"Her eyes are the color of the sky," said Reena, "but soon she will have the yellow eyes of the great hunter."

"And she will cry at the moon, as she cried for me from her den," said Teo.

The last light of day bathed the mountains in an orange glow as the hunters climbed the last path to the cave. Ohnka was the first inside. Wrapped in his heavy bearskin, he carried three ptarmigan, the fat white birds of the tundra, strung from his shoulder. The other men set their fresh game by the fire as they began preparations for the evening meal.

When everyone had gathered inside, Reena stood and spoke to Ohnka. "Teo has found a wolf child," she said.

A long silence passed as Ohnka stared at the sleeping cub that Teo held closely. "Take the wolf child outside," he said coldly. "The wolf brings only bad luck. It steals from our fires and casts evil spells on the valley. When the wolf is near, all the animals disappear and the hunting fails."

"But she will die," said Teo, his voice trembling. "There is no one to hunt for her."

"We have no food to share with the yellow-eyed thief," said Ohnka, still glaring at the cub. "She must leave."

"I can give her some of mine," said Teo, forgetting his fear.

"And some of mine," added Mova, who had been sitting quietly in the shadows.

Ohnka looked angrily at Mova. Ohnka was as strong and fearless as the cave lion, but Mova had the old eyes of wisdom, the eyes of the white owl.

"Teo needs a companion. He cannot be a hunter. The wolf child can stay with us when we break the stones," said Mova softly.

Ohnka relented. "She can stay until she's old enough to hunt for herself, until the first snow," he snapped. He turned and walked away. People hurried to make themselves busy.

"I can keep her, Mother," Teo said, bursting with excitement.

"Only until she's old enough to hunt," Reena reminded him. She looked at Mova, still sitting in his dark corner of the cave.

"Mova," said Teo, "will you really share your food?"

"I told you," he grumbled, "the wolf child is hungry."

After the evening meal Teo cuddled the wolf cub, close to the fire. Reena covered them with a warm blanket of fur and listened to the wind growling at the cave's mouth. Mova carefully lined up the stones for the next day's tools as Teo fell into a deep sleep filled with dreams of running across the Ice Mountain with the wolf child.

Teo and the wolf cub sat quietly watching Mova chip a large piece of flint. Teo had been up before dawn, stirring the fire and heating more of Reena's broth for the cub. As the deep blue of night gave way to the silvery morning, Ohnka and the men had gathered their weapons for the hunt, taking a meal of dried meat along. The women and children left soon after, carrying digging sticks and sacks of leather. Now the crisp light of day shone down on Mova as he showed Teo how to chip a spearhead from the lump of flint. With practiced strokes Mova hit the flint with a hammerstone, removing small chips, gradually revealing the desired shape. Mova stopped and examined the stone carefully, then struck hard at the top, chipping away a long, sharp flake that he would later bind to a strong stick with leather straps. He chipped another as Teo watched closely, remembering the sound. Mova motioned to Teo, handing him the hammerstone and a fresh piece of flint. The wolf cub sniffed at the stones as Teo laid them in his lap. He weighed the hammerstone, found a comfortable fit, and began to chip away the outer surface of the flint. It proved to be more difficult than it had seemed in Mova's swift demonstration, but the spearhead Teo formed was still sharp and useful, though much cruder looking than Mova's.

"You are learning to see the tools inside," said Mova.

"Perhaps the wolf child is bringing me luck," said Teo.

Mova grunted. "Only the wind can bring luck." He gathered the spearheads together. "Now we eat," he said, moving back into the cave.

Teo played with the cub as they ate their midday meal of dried meat and berries, then helped Mova carry a bundle of sticks to a warm perch in the sun. "How does the wind bring luck?" Teo asked as Mova began binding a newly made point to a spear shaft. Teo loved to hear stories of the great spirits. Long winter days were spent telling tales, singing songs, and acting out dramas of the world's beginnings. Mova set his work aside and moved closer.

"When the world was young," he began, "there was no wind. Snow fell straight down and piled up higher than mountains. That is how Great Lasa, the Ice Mountain, was born. There was no day, only the moon in the sky. In the darkness Ahmu, the first child, ran across the Ice Mountain to the place where the sky and land meet. He ripped a hole in the sky with his digging stick, and Nyac, the wind, came blowing through. She brought the birds of the air and the animals of the land, who gave the people gifts of food and clothing. Nyac blew the waters down the valleys, bringing the shining fish to the lakes. She sang with the voice of the great owl spirit and blew away the darkness to give us light. Ahmu ran to the first cave, and Nyac followed but would not enter. She did not blow out the first fire, but stayed outside and howled to keep the animals of sharp teeth and claws away. If the wind stops, the hunting is bad and the people will die. Nyac is good luck."

Mova's tale ended, and Teo knew he would not speak for a long while. Quietly Teo copied Mova's actions as he bound spearheads to shafts. The wolf cub slept peacefully at his side.

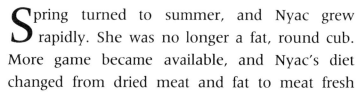

Spring turned to summer, and Nyac grew rapidly. She was no longer a fat, round cub. More game became available, and Nyac's diet changed from dried meat and fat to meat fresh from the hunt. Mova and Teo fed her from their shares. Teo and Nyac were inseparable. She slept close to Teo every night and waited patiently each day for him to finish making his tools. Then they would explore the rocky hillsides together.

"Nyac can run like the wind," Teo told Reena and Mova at the evening meal. "Today we chased Kewo across the slopes."

Reena laughed. "Kewo never stops running."

Nyac's eyes glowed in the flickering fire as Mova told the legend of Kewo, the lemming. "Each winter, white Kewo falls from the sky with the snowflakes. When summer burns hot, little Kewo turns brown and eats all the grass from the slope. Then Kewo changes into water and runs to the great shining lake and disappears."

Teo remembered the last lemming migration. Two years had passed, and now great fields of tall grass grew once more on the windy slopes. Thousands of holes dotted the land, homes for ground squirrels, hamsters, and mice. Herds of deer and horses browsed in the green pastures, and ducks and geese flocked to the marshes at the edge of the glacier lakes.

Teo and Nyac curled up by the fire. Reena covered them, patted Teo on the head, and stroked Nyac's thick fur. "They have become good friends," she said to Mova. He shared their fire now, having abandoned his dark corner when Nyac came.

"But soon the snow will come, and she must leave," said Mova quietly. "Ohnka will not forget."

Summer ended, and the wind sang through the woods at the foot of the mountains. Green leaves turned to orange and red, and the grasses dried to a golden yellow. Trout swam through the clear mountain streams, and great herds of reindeer traveled to the valleys in search of food. With them came the predators, the giant cats of the mountains.

As the seasons changed, so did Nyac. Taller and stronger, soon to be a full-grown wolf, she would growl softly at night if a cave lion or snow leopard prowled too near the mouth of the cave. Long before the people, she could hear the silent feet of the hungry animals. "She has strong magic," they would say. "She can hear the wind before it blows." They called Teo Keeper of the Wild Spirit, for Nyac was always at his side. They had never before lived with a wild animal and were amazed at how Nyac obeyed Teo's commands, how she came when called and seemed to understand his every word. Still curious and playful, she made friends with everyone in the cave—all except Ohnka. They called her Ahno-Nyac, "Magic Wind." But Ohnka refused to call her by name. "At first snowfall the wolf child must return to the wolves," he would say coldly, without looking at her.

The sun shone brightly through the clear autumn sky, and the air was cool and crisp as the wind blew from the frozen glacier. Overhead a flock of geese flew south to warmer lands. Teo raced Nyac to the rocky outcrop at the top of the hill. Nyac won easily. Teo sat next to her and caught his breath. "This is where I sat when you called," he said. Teo gazed down at the valley and remembered his anger on that day. Now he was proud to be a toolmaker, to be able to chip delicate points for the finest knives and needles.

Suddenly Nyac barked. There was a flash of color in the rocks below. "Stay here," Teo commanded. He crawled quietly down the gravel in time to see a little round hamster squeeze into its hiding place in the rocks. Then he reached out and picked up a stone.

"Nyac! Nyac!" he called.

The wolf scrambled across the rocks.

"I found it again," he said, and held out the perfect piece of obsidian he had thrown away many months before.

"It is the black stone," he said. "You helped me to find it. I will make a great spear." He hugged Nyac as she licked his chin. "Mova was right. Nyac is good luck."

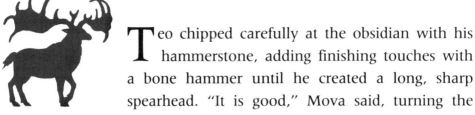

Teo chipped carefully at the obsidian with his hammerstone, adding finishing touches with a bone hammer until he created a long, sharp spearhead. "It is good," Mova said, turning the shiny black point over in his hands. "It will be a strong weapon with a powerful spirit."

"I will search the trees for the right piece of wood," said Teo, and called Nyac. Mova sat at the cave's mouth, still as an owl, watching them walk across the valley until they disappeared into the dark woods. The dense trees held back the wind, and the songs of the birds were the only sound Teo and Nyac could hear. They moved as silently as mice in tall grass, finding their secret path to the creek, stopping to drink from the icy water as it splashed over the glossy pebbles. Teo found a number of small saplings growing among the older trees and, selecting the straightest, cut it and stripped it of leaves. On returning to the edge of the woods, Nyac stopped short and perked up her ears.

"What is it, Nyac?" Teo asked. Fear gripped him as he crept forward. Vicious wild boar—more than a match for one wolf and a boy—roamed the woods in late autumn. Teo relaxed when he saw the giant elk step into the clearing. Cautioning Nyac to be still, he watched the beautiful animal move gracefully under the weight of its enormous antlers. A twig snapped under Teo's foot, and the elk swung its head to meet Teo's gaze. A ray of sunlight broke through the clouds of the gathering storm and bathed the elk's back in a golden glow. Then the elk turned and trotted across the open grassland.

Teo and Nyac watched until the elk was gone. Teo knew what the appearance of the first elk meant: The winter herds were beginning their migrations. "The giants of the Ice Mountain are coming," he told Nyac, thinking of the hairy beasts of the glacier. Though he had heard stories of them many times, he had never seen the musk ox, the woolly mammoth, or the woolly rhino. Only the elk would come close enough to enter the valley of the people. "The giants bring the snow with them," he said, looking toward the gray sky. Suddenly all was silent in the meadow as tiny snowflakes began drifting to earth. With a heavy heart Teo led Nyac back to the cave, for he knew that soon Ohnka would send her back to the wolves.

For three days it snowed, and on the fourth day the sky was clear and bright. Teo had busied himself with the making of the new spear, not wanting to think about Ohnka's decision. Now Ohnka stood over him, and Teo knew it was time.

"The wolf child must go," Ohnka said gruffly.

"Please let her stay. She is my friend," Teo pleaded. His eyes filled with tears, and Reena held him tightly.

"She has done no harm," she said.

"She must go," Ohnka said, glaring at them from under heavy brows. "She has the yellow eyes of the thief."

Tears spilled down Teo's cheeks as Mova stepped forward. "Nyac has strong magic," he said. "The hunts have been good since she came. She brings us luck."

"I have spoken," Ohnka said angrily, prodding Nyac with his heavy wooden club.

Nyac bared her teeth and snarled. Ohnka raised his club to strike, and Nyac lunged toward him.

"No!" screamed Teo, grabbing Nyac and holding her back.

"Teo!" Ohnka snapped. "Take Nyac outside! We leave now!"

Teo looked at Reena, who nodded. "She is old enough to feed herself. She will be all right," she said.

Mova knelt and looked into Nyac's yellow eyes. His gnarled hands quivered as he petted her gently. "Ahno-Nyac, friend of the cave," he said, "you must leave the Keeper of the Wild Spirit now and run like the wind across the Ice Mountain. You must find the wolves and sing with the voice of the great owl spirit."

A great sadness fell on the people of the cave as they watched Ohnka lead Teo and Nyac across the valley toward the wild, windswept plain beyond. They plunged ahead through great drifts of fresh snow that reached their knees. They stopped before a forest of tangled trees. Teo hugged Nyac. She licked his cheek and whined, sensing that something was wrong. "You can't live in the cave anymore," Teo said in a low whisper, his eyes wet with tears. "You must sleep with the wolves now. Be careful. The mountains are full of dangers." He wished there was more time as Ohnka motioned him to leave. Slowly Teo backed away, but Nyac followed.

"Go!" Teo yelled. "You can't come back!"

Nyac ran to him, leaping through the soft snow.

Ohnka raised his club in the air and chased Nyac into the woods, but she turned and came after Teo. Again Ohnka chased her, and again she followed, until finally he swung his heavy club in a great arc, chipping her painfully on the shoulder.

"Run, Nyac, run!" cried Teo.

Nyac stared at Teo for a moment in confusion, then turned and fled and disappeared into the shadows of the trees. As he followed Ohnka on the long way back to the cave, Teo thought his heart would break.

Three days passed. Teo spent hours gazing out of the cave's mouth, across the white valley, hoping for a sign of Nyac.

"She is gone, like the snow in springtime," Mova said, moving closer to the fire. "You must eat something, Teo," he said. "You must keep up your strength for the hunt."

When Teo and Ohnka had returned to the cave without Nyac, Ohnka had gathered everyone together. "In nine days we go to the Ice Mountain," he had said. "We will hunt the great mammoth." The people had begun talking all at once, some with excitement, others with fear. It had been years since they had marched to the glacier in search of the woolly mammoth. It would be a dangerous journey, and the whole tribe was needed.

Today everyone but Mova and Teo was in the woods, cutting long poles to carry their supplies. Teo glanced at the woods, then saw a tiny bit of gray move among the rocks in the distance. Nyac, he thought, and rushed from the cave.

"Nyac! Nyac!" he called. All was still. Then Teo's heart leaped as Nyac ran from behind the rocks and licked his chin. "Nyac, you've come back." Teo hugged her, feeling her ribs. "I will get you something to eat," he said. "Wait here," Teo ordered her as she began to follow. He returned with pieces of dried meat and followed Nyac high into the hills to the den where he had found her as a small cub. "Now you have your own cave," he said. "Ohnka must never find you." He remembered Ohnka's words: *If the wolf child returns, I will use my spear to stop her.* Teo told no one, keeping his secret even from Mova.

"Teo is glad to go on the hunt," said Reena as the day drew near, not understanding the true source of his happiness.

"Yes," said Mova. "He is making strong weapons and listens

to the stories again." Earlier in the day Mova had told Teo the legend of the woolly mammoth.

"Long ago Ahmu, the first child, lit a great fire. It melted the snows, and the Ice Mountain began to flow like a river. Tamir, the first mammoth, came to Ahmu. He told Ahmu he needed cold air to live, so Ahmu kept his fire inside the cave, and the Ice Mountain froze again. Then Tamir thanked Ahmu and returned home. Each winter Tamir blows white clouds of snow from his trunk and sends one mammoth as a gift to the people."

Teo learned how they used the hide of the mammoth for leather and the hair for rope, bones and ivory for tools, and meat and fat to feed on all winter.

Finally the night of the ceremony arrived. Teo felt the excitement grow as the people lit torches and walked single file deep into the cave. He had never before been inside the hunting room. It was used only on special occasions. Teo stared at the ceiling, which seemed to come alive in the flickering light. Painted horses danced above his head, herds of ibex and reindeer raced across the rock, and great elk battled each other with their twisted antlers. Teo's head spun with the powerful magic as he gazed at the last painting on the far wall. It was the giant shaggy beast of the glacier, the woolly mammoth, with its long grasping trunk and huge curved tusks of ivory.

A low rhythmic chanting began, first among the men, then among the women, as Ohnka called to the hunting spirits to bring them good luck. Mova set a pile of newly made spears by the fire. Each man would select a weapon to use for the mammoth. Ohnka reached down and chose Teo's spear, the spear of black obsidian. "This will be my weapon for Tamir's gift," he said. Teo smiled as Mova looked on proudly.

Snarling, with teeth bared, she ran straight for the mammoth.

The mammoth stepped back as the hunters reached it, torches blazing. It stamped its feet in rage, then turned in panic. They chased it to a ravine, where it fell to its death with a loud crash. This was the mammoth that would give its gift of bone and hide for this season.

As Ohnka looked on in disbelief, Nyac ran to Teo and licked his cheeks.

"Oh, Nyac," Teo said, his heart beating fast. "You saved our lives."

Ohnka stood over Teo and Nyac as the women climbed down the mountainside. "We will talk of the wolf child at the campfire tonight," Ohnka said, then ran to the aid of the hunters. Would he use his spear as he did on the mammoth, Teo wondered, or send Nyac away to freeze on the Ice Mountain?

Nyac stayed close as Teo silently helped Reena and the women prepare the mammoth for the long journey back. The hide was cleaned and laid flat, and meat was strapped to the long poles. By evening everything was hauled back to camp, where Mova and the children waited.

"Teo," said Mova, "tell me about the mammoth—and Nyac."

Nyac licked Mova's hand and sat at his knees while Teo told his story. "I was almost a spirit, Mova. The mammoth shook the ground when it ran. It had breath like fire and a voice like a hundred lions. It stood right over me and would have stepped on me if Nyac hadn't been there. She followed us from the cave and then ran like the wind to save me. She saved Ohnka, too."

Mova smiled as he petted Nyac.

Teo helped to light the fire for the celebration of the hunt, but his heart felt cold, for he knew that soon Ohnka would decide what to do with Nyac. The flames crackled as fresh wood was thrown in, and great billows of smoke were torn away by the freezing wind. Finally the fire died down to a pleasant warmth. The embers glowed brightly as the people huddled together to keep away the cold. A full silvery moon rose over the jagged mountains, and countless stars sparkled in the clear black night. Then Mova raised his hands to the sky, his hair glowing like the feathers of the white owl in the moonlight. The wind calmed to a gentle breeze as Mova began to speak.

"Long ago, before the winds blew away the night, Tamir, the mammoth, walked under the black sky. The moon was the only light. When its eye was open, Tamir could see the mountains, and the snows were bright; but when the moon shut its eye, all was dark. So Tamir blew great clouds of snowflakes higher and higher until they reached the sky. The snowflakes became the stars and stayed in the black night to light Tamir's way. The magic of the mammoth is strong."

As Teo gazed at the stars scattered across the sky, Ohnka spoke. "We thank you for your gift, Great Tamir," he said. "We have taken the mammoth. Now we return to the cave and leave you to roam the Ice Mountain." The people sang a song of praise to Tamir, their chanting echoing softly across the glacier valley.

Ohnka stood, and once again there was silence. Teo felt his heart beat loudly in his chest as he smoothed Nyac's fur with trembling hands.

"For many years we have come to the Ice Mountain for the mammoth," Ohnka said. "We have hunted bravely with fire and the pointed stones as our weapons." He stared at Nyac. "Today the wolf child attacked the mammoth," he said. Teo quivered, his arms around Nyac. Ohnka stared at the circle of people, his eyes shining like the great cave lion.

"The wolf child saved my life. She saved the life of Teo, Keeper of the Wild Spirit, and fought the mammoth with only her teeth as weapons. She is strong and brave and a friend to the people." Ohnka picked up a morsel of meat and knelt before Teo. "The bravest hunter gets the first piece of meat. This is for Ahno-Nyac, the hunter on four legs," he said, handing the morsel to Teo. "Nyac will stay with us and bring us good luck," Ohnka said with a smile as Nyac ate from Teo's hand.

The people laughed and began to chant a song of victory. Reena and Mova hugged Teo while Nyac threw her head back and howled long and high at the moon. "Mova," said Teo, "she sings with the voice of the great owl spirit." Everyone smiled at Nyac, who shook herself proudly. They sang deep into the night, scaring the spirits of the Ice Mountain far across the frozen valley. Teo and Nyac settled themselves, warm before the fire.

This story is set during the last Ice Age, over 18,000 years ago, when ice sheets up to two miles thick covered most of the Northern Hemisphere. Today the glaciers are gone, as is the way of life of the people who hunted across the frozen tundra. Gone, too, are the giant elk, the cave lion, the woolly rhinoceros, and the woolly mammoth. As the climate changed, the people learned to farm the land and raise animals for food, transportation, and companionship. In time they populated the earth, bringing the domesticated dog with them. Across a few isolated areas the last remaining wolves still run free, unchanged for millions of years. Humans are the wolves' only enemy, and their only friend. The wolf needs protection and understanding if it is to survive.